DATE DUE

DEMCO

greff

greff

The Story of a Guide Dog

BY PATRICIA CURTIS

PHOTOGRAPHS BY MARY BLOOM

LODESTAR BOOKS
E. P. Dutton   New York

LIBRARY OF CONGRESS CATALOGING IN PUBLICATION DATA
Curtis, Patricia.
    Greff, the story of a guide dog.

    Includes index.
    Summary: Traces the life of a Labrador retriever from birth through training at the Guide Dog Foundation, where he is introduced to the blind owner for whom he will be responsible.
    1. Guide dogs—Juvenile literature. 2. Greff (Dog)—Juvenile literature. 3. Guide dogs—Biography—Juvenile literature. [1. Guide dogs. 2. Labrador dogs. 3. Dogs] I. Bloom, Mary, ill. II. Title.
HV1780.S4C87   636.7'0886   81–23623
ISBN 0–525–66754–7 (Dutton)   AACR2

Published in the United States by E. P. Dutton, Inc., 2 Park Avenue, New York, N.Y. 10016.

Editor: Virginia Buckley   Designer: Trish Parcell
Printed in the U.S.A.   First edition
10   9   8   7   6   5   4   3   2

ACKNOWLEDGMENTS

We wish to thank the Guide Dog Foundation for the Blind, Inc., of Smithtown, New York, for their kind cooperation, which made this book possible. Our deepest appreciation goes to Joseph Capizzo, who was Greff's real-life trainer. He graciously allowed us to accompany him and take photographs as he worked, and he answered all our questions with patient good humor. Thanks also to Ernest M. Swanton, Executive Director, and to Emily Biegel, Director of Administrative Affairs—and to the entire staff, who helped us in so many ways in the preparation of this book.

PATRICIA CURTIS
MARY BLOOM

"I THINK KATE IS READY TO HAVE HER PUPPIES," announced Mrs. Troy, stroking the beautiful yellow Labrador retriever, whose bulging sides revealed that she was pregnant. It was a cool evening in early October, and normally Kate would have enjoyed a walk with a member of the family. But the dog seemed to want to stick close to home. Later that evening she went down to the warm basement, where a "whelping box"—a large open box lined with soft rags and clean newspapers—had been prepared for her.

When bedtime came, Mrs. Troy told her family good-night. "I think I'll sit up with Kate," she said. "I just have a feeling tonight's the night."

She made herself a pot of tea and sat down to wait in an old armchair beside the whelping box where Kate lay. Sure enough, shortly after midnight, Kate's puppies began to arrive. The first one born was a fine, sturdy little male. Then his seven brothers and sisters followed one by one. A few had some difficulty breathing at first, but Mrs. Troy rubbed their small backs, bathed them with warm water, or held them in her hands and moved them in a way that she knew would help them. Mrs. Troy had experience with newborn puppies, so she knew what to do.

Finally Kate settled down, looking contented. She washed her babies with her tongue. Their eyes and ears were tightly closed and they couldn't stand up, but instinctively they struggled to reach Kate's belly so they could begin to nurse. They mewed like baby kittens. First to reach his mother and attach himself to a nipple was the little firstborn male. His littermates followed. As Kate's milk began to flow, all eight tiny tails started to wag in unison.

Mrs. Troy watched them with satisfaction. "You pups don't know it yet, but some of you are going to lead very useful lives," she said.

Though she lived with the Troys, Kate and her puppies belonged to the Guide Dog Foundation, an organization that trains guide dogs for blind people. Kate herself had been entered in a training program, but the people at the Foundation had soon noticed that

she was unusually smart, sweet-tempered, and calm, as well as healthy and strong. She had all the qualities that make a perfect guide dog, so the director withdrew Kate from the training program in order to breed her. Everyone hoped that, with a guide dog as her mate, Kate would pass on those highly desirable qualities to her puppies, who would also become guide dogs.

The Troys had volunteered to have Kate live with them. All the female dogs that are singled out to become mothers live with families. The people at the Foundation believe that the puppies should be born and raised in private homes, not in kennels at the training center. Because they are loved and handled by people from the day they are born, the pups grow up to be friendly and sociable.

The little firstborn puppy was named Greff.

One afternoon about ten days after he was born, Greff's eyes and ears opened. He couldn't see very well for a few days, but gradually his eyes began to make out the shapes of his mother and littermates, the people who petted him, and the basement room that was his world so far.

Greff grew fat and strong. The puppies tumbled about, playing and wrestling with one another, climbing over their mother. Mr. Troy built a pen around the box to keep them from wandering around the basement and getting into trouble. When they became tired, they snuggled up together in a heap, so close that you couldn't tell where one pup left off and another began.

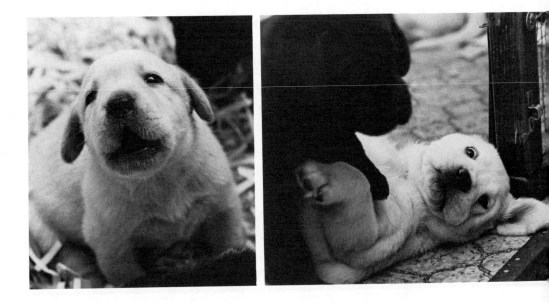

When they were about three weeks old, Kate decided it was time to wean her energetic, hungry brood—they were getting so big they wanted more to eat than she could give them. So Mrs. Troy started feeding the pups milk and cereal with additional vitamins in it. The pups made a mess of mealtimes at first. They climbed into their food dish and sat in their dinner, got it all over their faces, and dribbled it on the newspapers that covered the floor of their pen.

Soon they were allowed to play out in the sunshine, always with a member of the Troy family to supervise them. They waddled about exploring the enclosed yard—especially Greff, who was the bravest and most curious of the lot.

Then one day when Greff was about six weeks old, the first important change in his life took place. The Troys' doorbell rang, and Greff was suddenly picked up and kissed. He was put in a box by himself, carried to a car, and driven to another home. He didn't know it, of course, but the same thing happened to each of his brothers and sisters. Greff was taken to a family named McGovern, who were to be his "puppy walkers." When the Guide Dog Foundation's puppies are ready to leave their mother, they are separated. Each one goes to live with a family selected by the Foundation, where it will stay while it is growing up. These families, who are called puppy walkers, expose the puppies to as many different experiences as possible, so they learn to handle themselves in various life situations.

"Cindy and Mark, come and see our new puppy," called Mrs. McGovern as she lifted Greff out of his box. Her two little children came running to admire and stroke the puppy. "Gently, Mark," said the mother, for two-year-old Mark was hugging Greff too hard. The McGoverns' dog Ginger also came and sniffed at the bewildered puppy, as did their cat Whiskers.

Greff enjoyed all the petting and the games the McGoverns played with him, but when night came, that was a different story. He was taken to his box in a room by himself, patted good-night, and left alone in the dark. Suddenly he missed his mother and his brothers and sisters. What a wail he put up! Louder and

louder he howled. Several times Mrs. McGovern came
in to comfort him, but the minute she left, he began to
cry again. Then the door opened and a nice warm body
came in and settled down in the box with him. It was
Ginger. Still whimpering, the puppy crawled close to
her. Ginger licked him. Soon he fell asleep.

In the weeks that followed, Greff forgot about his
mother, his siblings, and the Troys. He was too busy
exploring his new home with all the interesting things
to do. His first order of business was to chew up as
many objects as possible—a pair of Cindy's socks, Mrs.
McGovern's slippers, one of Mr. McGovern's sneakers,
even one of Mark's diapers. Gradually he learned that
he should chew up only his own toys, and as he grew
older he stopped chewing up things altogether.

Life was pretty exciting for Greff. Cindy and Mark played with him. Mrs. McGovern brushed him regularly, so his coat grew healthy, thick, and shiny. He romped with Ginger in the fenced backyard and got lots of exercise. He enjoyed going with the family for rides in the car and never once was carsick.

When he was still a young puppy, he was taught to be clean in the house and to ask to go out when he had to relieve himself. He was scolded but never punished when he made mistakes in the house, and petted and praised when he did the right thing. Soon he got the idea that outdoors was the right place to go.

One early spring day, Mr. McGovern called Greff and took him for his first walk on the leash. Greff barked the whole time. What was this strange rope that Mr. McGovern was using to lead him or hold him back? But after a few walks, Greff decided that the leash wasn't so bad—in fact, he began to enjoy it. Even more exciting was his first trip to town. He was a little afraid of the trucks and cars, but all the people on the sidewalk seemed so nice and friendly that he soon forgot about the traffic in the street.

Once in a while, Greff was taken to the Guide Dog Foundation training center to visit. So many other dogs, such activity! There were rows of indoor cages, kennels with outdoor runs, and rooms where dogs were bathed and groomed. Trainers came and went with the dogs on leashes, taking them to and from the training sessions held on the grassy grounds behind the buildings. Several young helpers were busy brushing dogs, cleaning out cages, washing food bowls. Greff was excited and a little overwhelmed on these visits, but it was important that he get to know the place.

In April, when he was six months old, Mrs. McGovern enrolled Greff in obedience classes at the local Y. He was taught to come, sit, lie down, and stay—again, he was never punished for doing wrong but always praised warmly when he did well.

By the time he was a year old, Greff was a handsome, alert, confident, and friendly dog. It was time for his puppyhood to be over, time for real school to start.

One day a van pulled into the McGoverns' driveway. It was from the Guide Dog Foundation, and it had come to pick up Greff and take him to the training center, where he would live for the next five to seven months while he was taught everything he needed to know to guide a blind person.

"Good-bye, Greff," said the McGoverns, hugging him just as the Troy family had. They knew how much they would miss him—they had grown to love him.

Greff jumped eagerly into the van. He had no idea, of course, that he was leaving the McGovern family for good. When he got to the training center, he recognized it from previous visits. He became excited at seeing all the other dogs and the trainers and helpers.

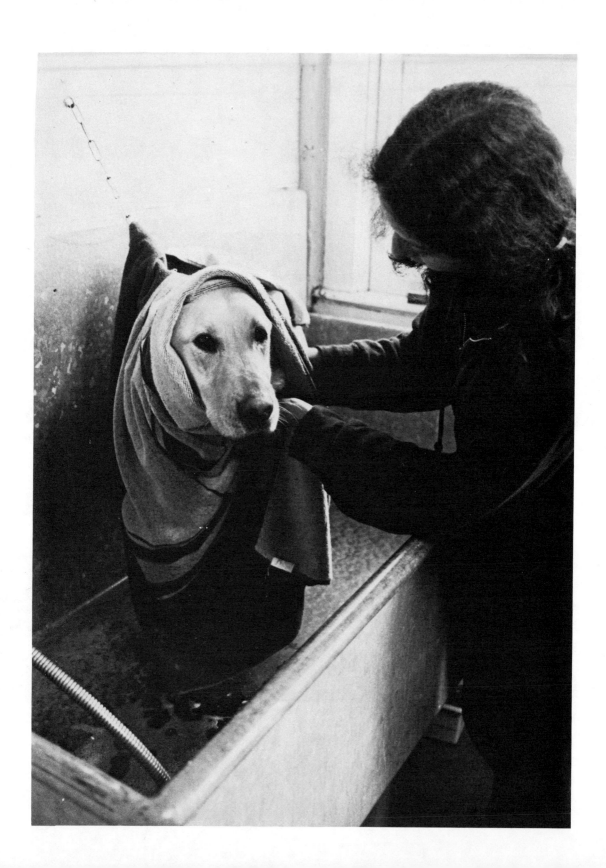

Elizabeth, the head trainer, came over to Greff and saw how alert and friendly he was. She patted him. "Greff, I think you will make a good guide dog," she said. Greff wagged his tail and licked Elizabeth's hand.

Greff enjoyed it when the helpers gave him a bath, brushed him, weighed and measured him, checked his teeth and ears. But when night came and he discovered he wasn't going home but would have to sleep in a cage all by himself, away from the other dogs there at the training center, he became depressed and homesick. His eyes took on a sad look, his head and tail drooped. He felt abandoned by his family.

The next day, a young man named Tom came and took Greff out of his cage and petted him. Tom was going to be Greff's trainer. He took Greff to the veterinarian for a thorough checkup and for medical tests, walked him, played with him. Greff liked Tom, and he began to cheer up. But again, when night came and he was left in his cage, Greff missed the McGoverns and Ginger.

After a few days, the training center got word from the vet that Greff's tests showed he was in perfect health. Now Greff was moved to a kennel where there were other dogs all around him. In the kennel next to him was a pretty German shepherd named Larkin, who took a liking to him and wanted to be friends. Affectionately she put her nose against Greff's cage, as if she wanted to talk to him. Larkin helped to cheer Greff up a bit.

Every day Tom put Greff on the leash and took him out on the grounds of the training center for his lessons. He taught Greff many new things. Greff learned to walk in a straight line beside Tom, always on Tom's left. He learned to stop whenever he came to a curb. When Tom said, "Hup hup!" and made a forward swing of his arm, Greff knew he was supposed to walk forward.

16

Tom took him out beside the road in front of the center and taught him to walk without being afraid of the traffic roaring by. On several occasions, Elizabeth came along and fired a cap pistol near Greff. It sounded like a car backfiring, and it was important that Greff learn not to flinch at such a noise. After a few times, Greff was no longer bothered by sudden bangs.

17

One day as Tom put Greff's collar and leash on him before going with him out on the grounds for his lessons, he added a harness with a tall handle.

"What's this funny thing?" Greff probably wondered, but it was not uncomfortable, so he didn't mind.

Tom petted him and told him what a fine dog he was. While they were walking briskly along the sidewalk, Greff suddenly became aware that Tom was not holding on to his leash but was holding the handle on the harness with his left hand.

"Wonder why he's doing that," Greff must have said to himself, but he was too busy concentrating on his lessons and didn't pay much attention to the new feeling.

B Braille Institute Library Services

Not all of Greff's time was devoted to lessons, however. Every afternoon when their work was over, Tom took Greff, Larkin, and two or three of the other dogs into the play yard. There they were free of the leashes and harnesses and could run and leap about, chase a ball, and play with one another, just like any young dogs having a good time. Greff loved those games.

Soon Greff's training became much more intense. One important lesson guide dogs have to learn is to watch for obstacles overhead, such as the branch of a tree, a low doorway, or an awning hanging over the sidewalk. If a guide dog were concerned only about himself, he could easily walk under the obstacle, but his blind owner would walk into it and get hurt. To teach guide dogs about overhangs, the training center has an obstacle course where poles are arranged overhead. The dogs are taught to lead the trainers around them.

Sometimes Tom put a blindfold on himself. Greff realized Tom walked differently then and that he had to do all the work of guiding, but he got used to it. He always tried to do what Tom wanted.

22

After several months of training, Greff was ready for his first trip to a shopping mall. He and Larkin and several other dogs went in the van with their trainers. The dogs were amazed at the lights and noise and crowds of people hustling by. Tom and Tony, Larkin's trainer, sat on a bench for about an hour and just let the dogs watch. Then they walked the dogs around the mall on their leashes, not in harness.

Suddenly Greff stopped in his tracks and began to growl. The hair on his back stood up. Tom was surprised—Greff had never growled at anything before. Then he saw what Greff was staring at. It was a little mechanical dog doing tricks in front of a shop. Greff crouched down and began to sneak up on it, still growling. Tom couldn't help laughing. When Tom laughed, Greff stopped growling, straightened up, wagged his tail, grinned, and barked. Greff seemed to be saying, "I was only kidding—I knew all along it is just a toy."

That day, Greff did one other thing he wasn't supposed to do. A young girl in the crowd stooped down to tie her shoe. Greff, walking by, turned his head and gave her a big slurpy kiss.

In the days that followed, Greff grew accustomed to stores, large buildings, stairways, elevators, swinging doors, shopping malls, railroad stations, bridges, and all the other places where a blind person might want to go. He also learned to walk right by other animals he met on the street—dogs, cats, pigeons, squirrels, and the like. When he was leading a blind owner someday, it would not do for Greff to want to stop and play or chase every other animal he met.

When Greff was in harness, leading Tom, he learned to keep himself between his trainer and other people or obstacles they passed. Greff and Tom even rode the subway. When they were in a restaurant, the dog learned to lie quietly under the table or under Tom's chair. (Although it is against the law for regular dogs to be in eating places, supermarkets, theaters, and many public buildings, guide dogs are permitted everywhere.)

The hardest lesson for Greff to learn was to ignore people who tried to pet him when he was in harness. People were attracted to the handsome yellow retriever, and Greff loved to be petted. But Tom taught him to concentrate only on working when he was in harness. Someday a blind person's life would depend on him.

Finally, it was spring again, and Greff was one and a half years old. He, Larkin, and the other dogs in their class were fully trained now and ready for their blind owners. One day, about a dozen blind people arrived at the training center. They were carrying suitcases, because they were going to stay for three weeks, getting to know their dogs, working with them, and learning to depend on them. While they were there, being taught by Elizabeth, Tom, and the other trainers, the blind people would be called students, even though they were grown men and women. Some of them had had dogs before who had become too old to be guide dogs and been given away as pets. Other blind students had never had dogs; sometimes the training was harder for them than it was for people getting their second or third dog. One young woman, a grade school teacher, was getting her first dog, whereas an older man was there to receive his seventh. But the training is essentially the same for everybody. Sometimes a person who has had a dog before has to unlearn some old habits before he or she can work well with a new dog.

26

The dogs were in their kennels while the blind students unpacked and got settled in the dormitory. The trainers already knew a great deal about the students from their letters of application and had formed some ideas about which dog would be most suitable for which person. Now that they had met the students, they discussed this subject again. It was very important to match the personality of a dog with the personality of an owner as closely as possible. The life-style and occupation of each person had to be considered, as well as his or her size—a small, elderly man, for example, should not receive an especially vigorous, powerful dog that he might have trouble walking with; instead he should be given a quieter, more lightly built dog. That evening, the trainers made their decisions, then went to the students and told them the names and characteristics of the dogs they would receive the next day. Out in the kennels, the dogs were restless. They sensed something was up.

Early the next morning, a young man named Peter awoke with a headache. He realized that the headache was from excitement. Peter, who had been blind since birth, had had a guide dog for many years who had recently been retired from work. Peter missed his dog a great deal, and he had flown alone across the United States to get a new dog.

Peter had graduated from public high school and now had a job in an office. He liked to take walks, listen to music, and to read books in Braille—a special method of printing where the letters are represented in raised dots on the pages, so that blind people can "read" them with their fingers. He had a girl friend back home named Sandra, who also was blind and had a guide dog. Peter had been told he would receive a yellow Labrador retriever named Greff.

After breakfast, Peter was left in a small room by himself—the trainers believe each student should be left alone with his or her dog for the first twenty minutes or so before they join the others, to get to know each other.

Peter waited. At last the door opened, and Tom led Greff up to him. "Okay, Peter, meet Greff," said Tom, handing Greff's leash to the student. "Greff, this is Peter." Then Tom went out and closed the door.

Peter reached out for Greff and put his arms around him. Greff stood wagging his tail and gazing with curiosity at the young man holding his leash.

"So you're going to be my dog, eh, Greff?" Peter sat down on the floor and ran his hands over Greff's body to feel what the dog looked like. Greff licked his face.

"I can tell you're going to be special," Peter said. He began to tumble and play with his dog. "Hey—let go of my arm! Easy!" Peter laughed as Greff pretended to bite his arm. Greff, in spite of all the hard work and everything he had learned, was still a lively and playful young dog.

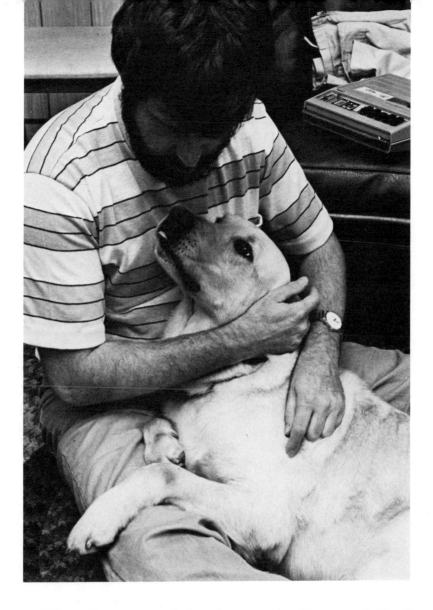

When Tom opened the door again, Peter and Greff were still sitting together on the floor, and Peter was talking calmly to his dog. "He is very sensitive to my voice," Peter reported happily. "He responds to whatever I tell him."

Peter and Greff went into the living room, where Peter told Greff to find him an empty seat. Greff took him to a chair next to the young schoolteacher, whose name was Jane. At Jane's feet lay her dog—Larkin.

Jane, like Peter, had always gone to public school. She had just graduated from college with a degree in education. "Wait till my kids see Larkin when I walk into my classroom next September!" she said. "I teach third and fourth grades, and of course my dog will always be in the classrooms with me. My children are fascinated by the fact that I'm blind and are always trying to help me. I told them I was getting a guide dog. They'll flip over Larkin." She fondled her dog's head and ears.

"How do you like your dog, Peter?" Jane asked.

"He's great, but my face is all sticky from being licked so much," Peter told her with a smile. "And after he kissed me, he batted his tail in my face. He's too much." He reached down and patted Greff, who was lying under his chair.

As soon as all the blind students had met their dogs and spent some time alone with them, Elizabeth gathered everybody together in the living room.

"Please practice walking around here in the dormitory with your dogs," she said. "Change seats, go back and forth to the bedrooms and into the dining room, pass one another in the hall. Always know where you're going and tell your dogs where to take you. Don't let them decide where to take you."

From that moment on, the blind owners took charge of their dogs. And just as the dogs had been taught to serve them, now the students had to learn how to take good care of their dogs. Peter fed Greff, filled his water bowl, brushed him, gave him a bath. Greff slept in a box on the floor near Peter's bed in the dormitory room. "When we get home, you can sleep *on* my bed, Greff," Peter whispered in his dog's ear.

During the next three weeks, Peter and Greff worked together every day. At first they walked around the grounds of the training center, then they ventured into the nearby town. A few days later they went to the

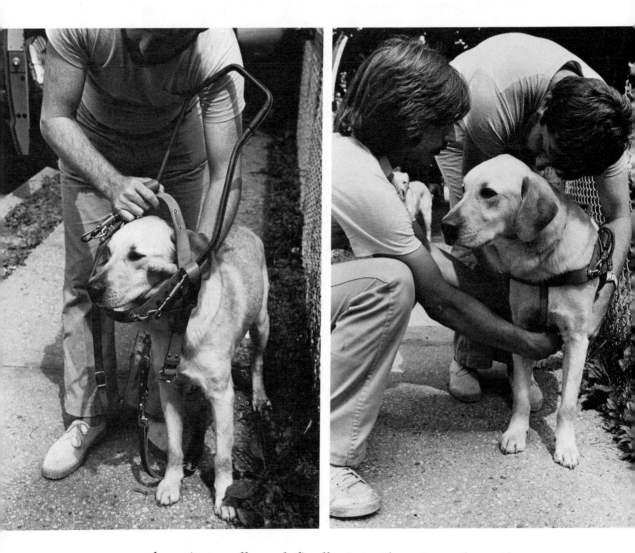

shopping mall, and finally into the city, where they even rode the subway. Tom was always with them, correcting their mistakes, offering advice to Peter.

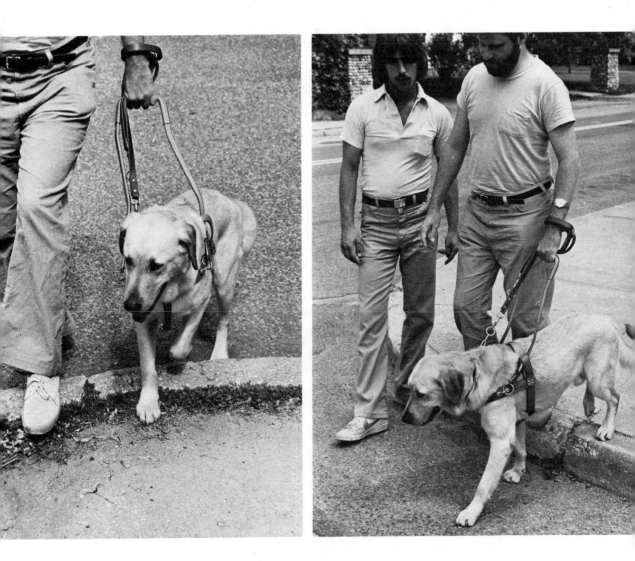

"Why does Greff have a tendency to pull me to the
right when we're walking?" Peter had asked Tom early
in his training with his dog.

"It's because you have an old habit of letting your left
arm extend too far forward," Tom had told him. "The
hand that's holding the handle should always be at

your side, about even with your pocket." Peter followed
Tom's advice and had no more trouble with the way
Greff led him.

"Greff is everything my other dog was and more," Peter told Jane after he had worked with the dog for several days.

At the end of every day, Peter played with Greff, tussling playfully with him and letting him run about the dormitory room. Life for Greff would never be all work and no fun.

One day after breakfast, Tom said to Peter, "Well, Pete, you and Greff are on your own today. I'll drive you into town or to the shopping mall, and you take it from there. Go where you want and get yourself back here."

Peter and Greff were gone for hours. Tom paced back and forth. Suppose something had happened to them? Greff was responsible for Peter's safety—suppose the dog made a bad mistake? "Is there anything I forgot to teach Greff?" Tom wondered. "Should I go and look for them?"

But just then, two figures could be seen walking toward the training center—a young man and a yellow Labrador retriever.

"Greff was great," reported Peter. "We had no problems. We even went into a coffee shop for lunch. Greff found a seat for me right away, and when I sat down, he lay down under my seat. He always stopped at curbs, he didn't shy at the traffic, and he zigzagged along the sidewalk when it was crowded so I wouldn't bump into anyone. Greff is more than I expected."

Jane went on her first trip alone with Larkin the next day. "Everything was fine except once when Larkin stopped and wanted to play with another dog," Jane said upon returning. "But when I corrected her, she got back to business right away."

Quickly the weeks of training together passed for Peter and Greff. It was clear that Greff knew he belonged to Peter and was responsible for him when he was in harness. And Peter felt confident that he could depend on Greff.

Peter bought a plane ticket home. Greff, of course, was going right in the cabin with him, lying under the seat. After they had been home for about a week, Tom would follow them to spend a few days giving "after care" on the spot—helping solve any problems that Greff and Peter might have encountered at home. It's hard to anticipate at the training center every situation that might arise once the blind person and his or her dog try to function in their own environment. Follow-up care by a trainer can help smooth out any problems.

But before Peter and Greff left the training center, there was graduation.

The day of graduation was sunny and warm, and chairs were set up on the lawn. Friends and relatives of the blind students began arriving early for the ceremony. Many people who had graduated in previous years also came with their dogs to join in the celebration. Peter and Jane, dressed in their best clothes, sat with the others in their class near the speakers.

The sun grew hot, and Peter began to worry that Greff would be thirsty and uncomfortable, but the dog never complained or tried to move away from Peter's chair. All the students received diplomas. Then it was time for Peter and Greff to catch their plane.

"Good-bye, Jane and Larkin," said Peter as he walked out of the dormitory. "Good luck to you." Tom was going to drive him and Greff to the airport.

Greff jumped into the car beside Peter. The little firstborn puppy had not only grown into a strong, intelligent, adult dog—he was a very well-trained animal who would greatly help a human being. Peter knew he could depend on Greff to guide him wherever he wanted to go. Peter and Greff both knew they could count on each other for something else—to be each other's good friend.

TRAINING CENTERS FOR GUIDE DOGS

The following facilities,
listed alphabetically by state,
train guide dogs for the blind:

International Guiding Eyes
5528 Cahuenga Boulevard
North Hollywood, California 91601
Phone: (213) 877–3937

Guide Dogs for the Blind
P.O. Box 1200
San Rafael, California 94902
Phone: (415) 497–4000

Fidelco Guide Dog Foundation
P.O. Box 142
Bloomfield, Connecticut 06002
Phone: (203) 243–5200

Leader Dogs for the Blind
1039 Rochester Road
Rochester, Michigan 48063
Phone: (313) 651–9011

The Seeing Eye
P.O. Box 375
Morristown, New Jersey 07960
Phone: (201) 539–4425

Guide Dog Foundation for the Blind
371 Jericho Turnpike
Smithtown, Long Island, New York 11787
Phone: (516) 265–2121

Guiding Eyes for the Blind
Granite Springs Road
Yorktown Heights, New York 10598
Phone: (914) 245–4024

Pilot Dogs
625 West Town Street
Columbus, Ohio 43215
Phone: (614) 221–6367

INDEX

ABOUT THE AUTHOR

PATRICIA CURTIS, a former editor at *Family Circle* magazine, is the author of *Cindy, A Hearing Ear Dog,* and three other books about animals. "I am especially fascinated by the bond between people and companion animals," she says. "I believe we are experiencing a slowly rising awareness of animals that will improve the ways people appreciate and treat them." Ms. Curtis lives in New York City.

ABOUT THE PHOTOGRAPHER

MARY BLOOM is an animal photographer who lives in New York City, where she frequently exhibits her photographs. A consultant to the A.S.P.C.A., she also works with unusual pets that have lived in people's homes, and tries to rehabilitate them back into a more natural environment.